"SATI SAVITRI: A TRUE STORY OF SELF-SACRIFICE AND COURAGE"

GOLU KUMAR

Contents

CHAPTER ONE

Sati savitri

Savitri was the only child
Of Madra's wise and mighty king;
Stern warriors, when they saw her, smiled,
As mountains smile to see the spring.
Fair as a lotus when the moon
Kisses its opening petals red,
After sweet showers in sultry June!
With a happier heart, and lighter tread,
Chance strangers, having met her, past,
And often would they turn the head
A lingering second look to cast,
And bless the vision ere it fled.
    What was her peculiar charm?
The soft black eyes, the raven hair,
The curving neck, the rounded arm,
All these are common everywhere.
Her charm was this--upon her face
Childlike and innocent and fair,
No man with thought impure or base
Could ever look;--the glory there,
The sweet simplicity and grace,
Abashed the boldest; but the good
God's purity there loved to trace,

Mirrored in dawning womanhood.
    In those far-off primeval days
Fair India's daughters were not pent
In closed zenanas. On her ways
Savitri at her pleasure went
Whither she chose,--and hour by hour
With young companions of her age,
She roamed the woods for fruit or flower,
Or loitered in some hermitage,
For the Munis gray and old
Her presence was as sunshine glad,
They taught her wonders manifold
And gave her the best they had.
    Her father let her have her way
In all things, whether high or low;
He feared no harm; he knew no ill
Could touch a nature pure as snow.
Long childless, as a priceless boon
He had obtained this child at last
By prayers, made morning, night, and noon
With many a vigil, many a fast;
Would Shiva his gift recall,
Or mar its perfect beauty ever?--
No, he had faith,--he gave her all
She wished, and feared and doubted never.
    And so she wondered where she pleased
In boyish freedom. Happy time!
No small vexations ever teased,
Nor crushing sorrows dimmed her prime.
One care alone, her father felt--
Where should he find a fitting mate
For one so pure?--His thoughts long dwelt
On this as with his queen he sat.

"Ah, whom, dear wife, should we choose?"
"Leave it to God," she answered and cried,
"Savitri may elect herself
Some day, her future lord and guide."
    Months passed, and lo, one summer morn
As to the hermitage, she went
Through smiling fields of waving corn,
She saw some youths in sports intent,
Sons of the hermits, and their peers,
And one among them tall and lithe
Royal in port,--on whom the years
Consenting, shed a grace so blithely,
So frank and noble, that the eye
Was loath to quit that sun-browned face;
She looked and looked,--then sighed,
And suddenly her pace slackened.
    What was the meaning--was it love?
Love at first sight, as poets sing,
Is then no fiction? Heaven above
Is witness, that the heart its king
Finds often like a lightning flash;
We play,--we jest,--we have no care,--
When hark a step,--there comes no crash,--
But life, or silent slow despair.
Their eyes just met,--Savitri past
Into the friendly Muni's hut,
Her heart rose had opened at last--
Opened no flower can ever shut.
    In converse with the gray-haired sage
She learned the story of the youth,
His name and place and parentage--
Of royal race, he was in truth.
Satyavan was he hight,--his sire

Dyoumatsen had been Salva's king,
But old and blind, opponents dire
Had gathered round him in a ring
And snatched the scepter from his hand;
Now,---with his queen and only son
He lived as a hermit in the land,
And gentler hermit was their none.
    Many tears were said and heard
The story,--and with praise sincere
Of Prince Satyavan; every word
Sent up a flush on cheek and ear,
Unnoticed. Hark! The bells remind
'Tis time to go,--she went away,
Leaving her virgin heart behind,
And richer for the loss. A ray,
Shot down from heaven, appeared to tinge
All objects with supernal light,
The thatches had a rainbow fringe,
The cornfields looked more green and bright.
    Savitri's first care was to tell
Her mother all her feelings new;
The queen her fears to dispel
To the king's private chamber flew.
"Now what is it, my gentle queen,
That makes thee hurry in this wise?"
She told him, smiles and tears between,
All she had heard; was the king with sighs
Sadly replied:--"I fear me much!
When is his race and what is his creed?
Not knowing aught, can we in such
A matter delicate, proceed?"
    As if the king's doubts to allay,
Came Narad Muni to the place

A few days after. Old and gray,
All loved to see the gossip's face,
Great Brahma's son,--adored of men,
Long absent, doubly welcome he
Unto the monarch, hoping then
With his assistance, clear to see.
No god in heaven, nor king on earth,
But Narad knew his history,--
The sun's, the moon's, the planets' birth
Was not to him a mystery.
"Now welcome, welcome, dear old friend,
All hail, and welcome once again!"
The greeting had not reached its end,
When glided like a music-strain
Savitri's presence throughout the room.--
"And who is this bright creature, say,
Whose radiation lights the chamber's gloom--
Is she an Apsara or fay?"
"No son thy servant hath, alas!
This is my one,--my only child;"--
"And married?"--"No."--"The season's passed,
Make haste, O king,"--he said, and smiled.
"That is the very theme, O sage,
In which thy wisdom ripe I need;
Seen hath she at the hermitage
A youth to whom in very deed
Her heart inclines."--"And who is he?"
"My daughter, tell his name and race,
Speak as to men who love thee."
She turned to them her modest face,
And answered quietly and clearly.--
"Ah, no! ah, no!--It cannot be--
Choose out another husband, dear,"--

The Muni cried,--"or woe is me!"
"And why should I? When I have given
My heart away, though but in thought,
Can I take it back? Forbid it, Heaven!
It was a deadly sin, I wot.
And why should I? I know no crime
In him or his."--"Believe me, child,
My reasons shall be clear in time,
I speak not like a madman wild;
Trust me in this."--"I cannot break
A plighted faith,--I cannot bear
A wounded conscience."--"Oh, forsake
This fancy hence may spring despair."--
"It may not be."--The father heard
By turns the speakers, and in doubt
Thus interposed a gentle word,--
"Friend should friend his mind speak out,
Is he not worthy? tell us."--"Nay,
All worthiness is in Satyavan,
And no one can my praise gainsay:
Of solar race--more god than man!
Great Soorasen, his ancestor,
And Dyoumatsen his father blind
Are known to fame: I can ever
No kings have been so good and kind."
"Then where, O Muni, is the bar?
If wealth be gone, and kingdom lost,
His merit remains a star,
Nor melts his lineage like the frost.
For riches, worldly power, or rank
I care not,--I would have my son
Pure, wise, and brave,--the Fates I thank
I see no hindrance, no, not one."

"Since thou insistest, King, to hear
The fatal truth,--I tell you,--I,
Upon this day as rounds the year
The young Prince Satyavan shall die."
This was enough. The monarch knew
The future was no sealèd book
To Brahma's son. A clammy dew
Spread on his brow,--he gently took
Savitri's palm in his, and said:
"No child can give away her hand,
A pledge is not unsanctionèd;
And here, if right I understand,
There was no pledge at all,--a thought,
A shadow,---barely crossed the mind--
Unblamed, it may be clean forgot,
Before the gods, it cannot bind.
"And think upon the dreadful curse
Of widowhood; the vigils, fasts,
And penances; no life is worse
Then hopeless life,--the while it lasts.
Day follows a day in one long round,
Monotonous and blank and dear;
Less painful was it to be bound
On some bleak rock, for aye to hear--
Without one chance of getting free--
The ocean's melancholy voice!
Mine be the sin,--if sin there be,
But tho must make a different choice."
In the meek grace of virginhood
Unblanched her cheek, undimmed her eye,
Savitri, like a statue, stood,
Somewhat austere was her reply.
"Once, and once only, all submit

To Destiny,--'tis God's command;
Once, and once only, so 'tis writ,
Shall woman pledge her faith and hand;
Once, and once only, can a sire
Unto his well-loved daughter say,
In presence of the witness fire,
I give thee to this man away.
"Once, and once only, have I given
My heart and faith--'tis past recall;
With conscience, none have ever striven,
And none may strive, without a fall.
Not the less solemn was my vow
Because unheard, and oh! the sin
Will not be less, if I should now
Deny the feeling felt within.
Unwedded to my dying day
I must, my father dear, remain;
'Tis well, if so thou willest, but say
Can man balk Fate, or break its chain?
"If Fate so rules, that I should feel
The miseries of a widow's life,
Can man's device the doom repel?
Unequal seems to be strife,
Between Humanity and Fate;
None have on earth what they desire;
Death comes to all or soon or late;
And peace is but a wandering fire;
Expediency leads wild astray;
The Right must be our guiding star;
Duty our watchword, come what may;
Judge for me, friends,--as wiser far."
She said and meekly looked at both.
The father, though the patient heard,

To give the sanction still seemed loth,
But Narad Muni took the word.
"Bless thee, my child! 'Tis not for us
To question the Almighty will,
Though cloud on cloud loom ominous,
In gentle rain, they may distill."
At this, the monarch--"Be it so!
I sanction what my friend approves;
All praise to Him, to whom praise we owe;
My child shall wed the youth she loves."
    Great joy in Madra. Blow the shell
The marriage over to declare!
And now to forest shades where dwell
The hermits, wend the wedded pair.
The doors of every house are hung
With gay festoons of leaves and flowers;
And blazing banners broad are flung,
And trumpets blown from castle towers!
Slow the process makes its ground
Along the crowded city street:
And blessings in a storm of sound
At every step the couple greets.
    Past all the houses, past the wall,
Past gardens gay, and hedgerows trim,
Past fields, where sinuous brooklets small
With molten silver to the brim
Glance in the sun's expiring light,
Past Frowning Hills, Past Pastures Wild,
At last, arises on the sight,
Foliage on foliage densely piled,
The woods are primeval, where reside
The holy hermits;--henceforth here
Must live the fair and gentle bride:

But this thought brought with it no fear.
Fear! With her husband by her still?
Or weariness! Where all was new?
Hark! What a welcome from the hill!
There are gathered hermits few.
Screaming the peacocks upward soar;
Wondering the timid wild deer gaze;
And from Briarean fig trees hoar
Look down at the monkeys in amaze
As the procession moves along;
And now behold, the bridegroom's sire
With joy comes forth amid the throng;--
What reverence his looks inspire!
Blind! With his partner by his side!
For them, it was a hallowed time!
Warmly they greet the modest bride
With her dark eyes and front sublime!
One only grief they feel.--Shall she
Who dwelt in palace halls before,
Dwell in their huts beneath the tree?
Would not their hard life press her sore;--
The manual labor and they want
Of comforts that her rank became,
Varkala robes, meals poor and scant,
Do all undermine the fragile frame?
To see the bride, the hermits' wives
And daughters gathered to the huts,
Women of pure and saintly lives!
And there beneath the betel-nuts
Tall trees like pillars, they admire
Her beauty, and congratulate
The parents, that their hearts' desire
Had thus accorded by Fate,

And Satyavan their son had found
In exile loan, a fitting mate:
And gossips add,--good signs abound;
Prosperity shall on her wait.
    Good signs in features, limbs, and eyes,
That old experience can discern,
Good signs on earth and in the skies,
That it could read at every turn.
And now with rice and gold, all bless
The bride and bridegroom,--and they go
Happy in others' happiness,
Each to her home, beneath the glow
Of the late risen moon that lines
With silver, all the ghost-like trees,
Sals, tamarisks, and South-Sea pines,
And palms whose plumes wave in the breeze.
    False was the fear, the parents felt,
Savitri liked her new life much;
Though in a lowly home she dwelt
Her conduct as a wife was such
As to illumine all the place;
She sickened not, nor sighed, nor pined;
But with simplicity and grace
Discharged each household duty kind.
Strong in all manual work,--and strong
To comfort, cherish, help, and pray,
The hours passed peacefully along
And rippling bright, day followed day.
    At morn Satyavan to the wood
Early repaired and gathered flowers
And fruits, in their wild solitude,
And fuel,--till advancing hours
Apprised him that his frugal meal

Awaited him. Ah, happy time!
Savitri, who with fervid zeal
Had said her orisons sublime,
And fed the Bramins and the birds,
Now ministered. Arcadian love,
With tender smiles and honeyed words,
All bliss of earth thou art above!
    And yet there was a specter grim,
A skeleton in Savitri's heart,
Looming in shadow, somewhat dim,
But which would never then depart.
It was that fatal, fatal speech
Of Narad Muni. As the days
Slip smoothly past, each after each,
In private she prays more fervent.
But there is none to share her fears,
How could she communicate
The sad cause of her bidden tears?
The doom approached the fatal date.
    No help from man. Well, be it so!
No sympathy,--it matters not!
God can avert the heavy blow!
He answers worship. Thus she thought.
And so, her prayers, by day and night,
Like incense rose unto the throne;
Nor did she vow neglect or rite
The Vedas enjoin or helpful own.
Upon the fourteenth of the moon,
As nearer came the time of dread,
In Joystee, that is May or June,
She vowed her vows and Bramins fed.
    And now she counted e'en the hours,
As to Eternity they passed;

O‘er head the dark cloud darker lowers,
The year is rounding full at last.
To-day,--to-day,--with doleful sound
The word seemed in her ear to ring!
O breaking heart,--thy pain profound
Thy husband knows not, nor the king,
Exiled and blind, nor yet the queen;
But One knows in His place above.
To-day,--to-day,--it will be seen
Which shall be victor, Death or Love!
Incessant in her prayers from morn,
The noon is safely tided,--then
A gleam of faint, faint hope is born,
But the heart fluttered like a wren
That sees the shadow of the hawk
Sail on,--and trembles in affright,
Lest a down-rushing swoop should mock
Its fortune, and overwhelm it quite.
The afternoon has come and gone
And brought no change;--should she rejoice?
The gentle evening shades come on,
When to hark!--She hears her husband’s voice!
"The twilight is most beautiful!
Mother, to gather fruit I go,
And fuel,--for the air is cool
Expect me in an hour or so."
"The night, my child, draws on apace,"
The mother’s voice was heard to say,
"The forest paths are hard to trace
In the darkness,--till the morrow stay."
"Not hard for me, who can discern
The forest paths in an hour,
Blindfold I could with ease return,

And the day has not yet lost its power."
"He goes then," thought Savitri, "thus
With unseen bands Fate draws us on
Unto the place appointed us;
We feel no outward force,--anon
We go to marriage or death
At a determined time and place;
We are her playthings; with her breath
She blows us where she lists in space.
What is my duty? It is clear,
My husband, I must follow; so,
While he collects his forest gear
Let me get permission to go."
His sire she seeks,--the blind old king,
And asks him permission straight.
"My daughter, night with ebon wing
hovers above; the hour is late.
My son is active, brave, and strong,
Conversant with the woods, he knows
each path; methinks it would be wrong
For thee to venture where he goes,
Weak and defenseless as thou art,
At such a time. If tho wert near
Thou mightst embarrass him, dear heart,
Alone, he would not have a fear."
So spake the hermit-monarch blind,
His wife too, entering in, express
The self-same thoughts in words such as kind,
And begged Savitri hard, to rest.
"Thy recent fasts and vigils, child,
Make thee unfit to undertake
This journey to the forest wild."
But nothing could shake her purpose.

She urged the nature of her vows,
Required her now the rites were done
To follow where her loving spouse
Might even be a chance of danger running.
"Go then, my child,--we give thee leave,
But with thy husband's quick return,
Before the flickering shades of eve
Deepen tonight, and planets burn,
And forest paths become obscure,
Lit only by their doubtful rays.
The gods, who guard all women pure,
Bless thee and kept thee in thy ways,
And safely bring thee and thy lord!"
On this, she left and swiftly ran
Where with his saw instead of a sword,
And basket plodded Satyavan.
Oh, lovely are the woods at dawn,
And lovely in the sultry noon,
But loveliest, when the sun withdrawn
The twilight and a crescent moon
Change all asperities of shape,
And tone all colors softly down,
With a blue veil of silvered crape!
Lo! By that hill which palm trees crown,
Down the deep glade with perfume rife
From buds, that to the dews expand,
The husband and the faithful wife
Pass to dense jungle,--hand in hand.
Satyavan bears beside his saw
A forkèd stick to pluck the fruit,
His wife, the basket lined with straw;
He talks, but she is almost mute,
And very pale. The minutes pass;

The basket has no further space,
Now on the fruits they flowers amass
That with their red flush all the place
While twilight lingers; then for wood
He saws the branches of the trees,
The noise heard in the solitude,
Grates on its soft, low harmonies.
    And all the while one dreadful thought
Haunted Savitri's anxious mind,
Which would have fain its stress forgot;
It came as chainless as the wind,
Of and again: thus on the spot
Marked with his heart-blood of comes back
The murdered man, to see the clot!
Death's final blow,--the fatal wreck
Of every hope, when will it fall?
For fall, by Narad's words, it must;
Persistent rising to appeal
This thought its horrid presence thrust.
    Sudden the noise is hushed,--a pause!
Satyavan lets the weapon drop--
Too well Savitri knows the cause,
He feels not well, the work must stop.
Pain is in his head,--a pain
As if he felt the cobra's fangs,
He tries to look around,--in vain,
A mist before his vision hangs;
The trees whirl dizzily around
In a fantastic fashion wild;
His throat and chest seem iron-bound,
He staggers, like a sleepy child.
    "My head, my head!--Savitri, dear,
This pain is frightful. Let me lie

Here on the turf." Her voice was clear
And very calm was her reply,
As if her heart had banned fear:
"Lean, love, thy head upon my breast,"
And as she helped him, added--"here,
So shall tho better breathe and rest."
"Ah me, this pain,--'tis getting dark,
I see no more,--can this be death?
What means this, gods?--Savitri, mark,
My hands wax cold, and fails my breath."
"It may be but a swoon." "Ah! no--
Arrows are piercing through my heart,--
Farewell, my love! for I must go,
This, this is death." He gave one start
And then lay quiet on her lap,
Insensitive to sight and sound,
Breathing his last... The branches flap
And fireflies glimmer all around;
His head upon her breast; his frame
The part on her lap, the part on the ground,
Thus lies he. Hours pass. Still the same,
The pair look statues, magic-bound.
Death in his palace holds his court,
His messengers move to and fro,
Each of his mission makes a report,
And takes the royal orders,--Lo,
Some slow before his throne appear
And humbly in the Presence kneel:
"Why hath the Prince not been brought here?
The hour is past; nor is an appeal
Allowed against foregone decree;
There is the mandate with the seal!
How comes it ye return to me

Without him? Shame upon your zeal!"
"O King, whom all men fear,--he lies
Deep in the dark Medhya wood,
We fled from then in wild surprise,
And left him in that solution.
We dare not touch him, for there sits,
Beside him, lighting all the place,
A woman fair, whose brow permits
In its austerity of grace
And purity,--no creatures foul
As we seemed, by her loveliness,
Or soul of evil, ghost or ghoul,
To venture close, and far, far less
"To stretch a hand, and bear the dead;
We left her leaning on her hand,
Thoughtful; no tear-drop had she shed,
But looked the goddess of the land,
With her meek air of mild command."--
"Then on this errand, I must go
Myself, and bear my dreaded brand,
This duty unto Fate I owe;
I know the merits of the prince,
But merit saves not from the doom
Common to man; his death long since
Was destined in his beauty's bloom."
As still, Savitri sat beside
Her husband dying,--dying fast,
She saw a stranger slowly glide
Beneath the boughs that shrunk aghast.
Upon his head, he wore a crown
That shimmered in the doubtful light;
His vestment scarlet reached low down,
His waist, a golden girdle diet.

His skin was dark as bronze; his face
Irradiate, and yet severe;
His eyes had much love and grace,
But glowed so bright, they filled with fear.
    A string was in the stranger's hand
Noosed at its end. Her terrors now
Savitri scarcely could command.
Upon the sod beneath a bough,
She gently laid her husband's head,
And in obeisance bent her brow.
"No mortal form is thin,"--she said,
"Beseech thee say what god art thou?
And what can be thin errand here?"
"Savitri, for thy prayers, thy faith,
Thy frequent vows, thy fasts severe,
I answer,--list,--my name is Death.
    "And I am come myself to take
Thy husband from this earth away,
And he shall cross the doleful lake
In my charge, and let me say
Too few such honors, I accord,
But his pure life and thin require
No less from me." The dreadful sword
Like lightning glanced one moment direly;
And then the inner man was tied,
The soul no bigger than the thumb,
To be borne onwards by his side:--
Savitri all the while stood dumb.
    But when the god moved slowly on
To gain his dominion dim,
Leaving the body there--anon
Savitri meekly followed him,
Hoping against all hope; he turned

And looked surprised. "Go back, my child!"
Pale, pale the stars above them burned,
Weirder the scene had grown wild;
"It is not for the living--hear!
To follow where the dead must go,
Thy duty lies before the clear,
What thou shouldst do, the Shasters show.
"The funeral rites that they ordain
And sacrifices must take up
Thy first sad moments; not in vain
Is held to thee this bitter cup;
Its lessons thou shall learn in time!
All that thou _canst_ do, thou hast done
For thy dear lord. Thy love sublime
My deepest sympathy hand won.
Return, for tho hast, come as far
As a living creature may. Adieu!
Let duty be thy guiding star,
As ever. To thyself be true!"
"Where'er my husband dear is led,
Or journeys of his own free will,
I too must go, though darkness spread
Across my path, portending ill,
'Tis thus my duty I have read!
If I am wrong, oh! with me bear;
But do not bid me backward tread
My way forlorn,--for I can dare
All things but that; ah! pity me,
A woman frail, too sorely tried!
And let me follow thee,
O graceful god,--whatever betide.
"By all things sacred, I entreat,
By Penitence that purifies,

By prompt Obedience, full, complete,
To spiritual masters, in the eyes
Of gods so precious, by the love
I bear my husband, by the faith
That looks from earth to heaven above,
And by thy own great name O Death,
And all thy kindness, bid me not
To leave thee, and to go my way,
But let me follow as I ought
Thy steps and his, as best I may.
"I know that in this transient world
All is delusion,--nothing true;
I know its shows are mists unfurled
To please and vanish. To renew
Its bubble joys, be magically bound
In _Maya's_ network frail and fair,
Is not my aim! The gladsome sound
Of husband, brother, friend, is air
To such as know that all must die,
And that at last, the time must come,
When eye shall speak no more to eye
And Love cry,--Lo, this is my sum.
"I know in such a world as this
No one can gain his heart's desire,
Or pass the years in perfect bliss;
Like gold we must be tried by fire;
And each shall suffer as he acts
And thinks,--his sad burden bear;
No friends can help,--his sins are facts
That nothing can annul or square,
And he must bear their result.
Can I save my husband by rites?
Ah, no,--that was a vain pretense,

Justice eternal strict requites.
"He for his deeds shall get his due
As I for mine: thus here each soul
Is its friend if it pursues
The right, and run straight for the goal;
But it's own worst and direst foe
If it chooses evil, and in tracks
Forbidden, for its pleasure, go.
Who knows not this, lacks true wisdom,
Virtue should be the turn and end
Of every life, all else is vain,
Duty should be its dearest friend
If higher life, it would attain."
"So sweet thy words ring on mine ear,
Gentle Savitri, that I feel
Would give some signs to make it clear
Thou hast not prayed to me in vain.
Satyavan's life I may not grant,
Nor take before its term thy life,
But I am not all adamant,
I feel for thee, thou faithful wife!
Ask thou aught else, and let it be
Some good thing for thyself or thin,
And I shall give it, child, to thee,
If any power on earth be mine."
"Well be it so. My husband's sire,
Hath lost his sight and fair domain,
Give to his eyes their former fire,
And place him on his throne again."
"It shall be done. Go back, my child,
The hour wears late, the wind feels cold,
The path becomes more weird and wild,
Thy feet are torn, there's blood, behold!

Thou feelest faint from weariness,
Oh try to follow me no more;
Go home, and with thy presence bless
Those who thin absence there deplore."
"No weariness, O Death, I feel,
And how should I, when by the side
Of Satyavan? In woe and weal
To be a helpmate swears the bride.
This is my place; by solemn oath
Wherever thou conductest him
I too must go, to keep my troth;
And if the eye at times should brim,
'Tis human weakness, give me strength
My work appointed to fulfill,
That I may gain the crown at length
The gods give those who do their will.
"The power of goodness is so great
We pray to feel its influence
Forever on us. It is late,
And the strange landscape awes my sense;
But I would fain with the goon,
And hear thy voice so true and kind;
The false lights on objects shone
Have vanished, and no longer blind,
Thanks to thy simple presence. Now
I feel a fresher air around,
And see the glory of that brow
With flashing rubies fitly crowned.
"Men call thee Yama--conqueror,
Because it is against their will
They follow thee,--and they abhor
The Truth which thou wouldst aye instill.
If they thy nature knew right,

Oh God, all other gods above!
And that thou conquerest in the fight
By patience, kindness, mercy, love,
And not by devastating wrath,
They would not shrink in childlike fright
To see thy shadow on their path,
But hail thee as sick souls the light."
"Thy words, Savitri, greet mine ear
As sweet as fountains that murmur low
To one who in the deserts fear
With parchèd tongue moves faint and slow,
Because thy talk is heart-sincere,
Without hypocrisy or guile;
Demand another boon, my dear,
But not of those forbad erewhile,
And I shall grant it, ere we part:
Lo, the stars pale,--the way is long,
Receive thy boon, and homewards start,
For ah, poor child, thou art not strong."
"Another boon! My sire the king
Besides myself hand children none,
Oh grant that from his stock may spring
A hundred boughs." "It shall be done.
He shall be blest with many a son
Who his old palace shall rejoice."
"Each heart-wish from thy goodness won,
If I am still allowed a choice,
I fain thy voice would ever hear,
Reluctant am I still to part,
The way seems short when thou art near
And Satyavan, my heart's dear heart.
"Of all the pleasures given on earth
The company of the good is best,

For weariness has never birth
In such commerce sweet and blest;
The sun runs on its wonted course,
The earth its plenteous treasure yields,
All for their sake, and by the force
Their prayer united ever wields.
Oh let me ever dwell
Amidst the good, wherever it be,
Whether in lowly hermit-cell
Or in some spot beyond the sea.
    "The favors man accords to men
Are never fruitless, from the rise
A thousand acts beyond our ken
That float like incense to the skies;
For benefits can ne'er effect,
They multiply and spread widely,
And honor follows on their trace.
Sharp penances and vigils dread,
Austerities, and wasting fasts,
Create an empire, and the blister
Long as this spiritual empire lasts
Become the saviors of the rest."
    "O thou endowed with every grace
And every virtue,--thou whose soul
Appears upon thy lovely face,
May the great gods who have all control
Send them their peace. I too would give
One favor more before I go;
Ask something for yourself, and live
Happy, and dear to all below,
Till summoned to the bliss above.
Savitri asks, and ask unblamed."--
She took the clue, felt Death was Love,

For no exceptions now he named,
And boldly said,--"Thou knowest, Lord,
The inmost hearts and thoughts of all!
There is no need to utter a word,
Upon thy mercy sole, I call.
If speech be needful to obtain
Thy grace,--oh hear a wife forlorn,
Let my Satyavan live again
And children unto us be born,
Wise, brave, and valiant." "From thy stock
A hundred families shall spring
As lasting as the solid rock,
Each son of thin shall be a king."
As thus he spoke, he loosed the knot
The soul of Satyavan that bound,
And promised further that their lot
In pleasant places should be found
Thenceforth, and that they both should live
For four centuries, to which the name
Of fair Savitri, men would give,--
And then he vanished in a flame.
"Adieu, great god!" She took the soul,
No bigger than the human thumb,
And running swift, soon reached her goal,
Where lay the body stark and dumb.
She lifted it with eager hands
And as before, when he expired,
She placed the head upon the bands
That bound her breast which hopes new-fired,
And which alternate rose and fell;
Then placed his soul upon his heart
Whence like a bee it found its cell,
And lo, he woke with a sudden start!

His breath came low at first, then deep,
With an unquiet look, he gazed,
As one waking from a sleep
Wholly bewildered and amazed.
As consciousness came slowly back
He recognized his loving wife--
"Who was it, Love, through regions black
Where hardly seemed a sign of life
Carried me bound? Methinks I view
The dark face yet-- a noble face,
He had a robe of scarlet hue,
And ruby crown; far, far through space
He bore me, on and on, but now,"--
"Thou hast been sleeping, but the man
With glory on his kingly brow,
Is gone, thou seest, Satyavan!
"O my belovèd,--thou art free!
Sleep which had bound thee fast, hand left
Thin eyelids. Try yourself to be!
For late of every sense beret
Thou seemest in a rigid trance;
And if thou canst, my love, arise,
Regarding the night, the dark expanse
Spread out before us, and the skies."
Supported by her, looked at him long
Upon the landscape dim outspread,
And like some old remembered song
The past came back,--a tangled thread.
"I had pain as if an asp
Gnawed in my brain, and there I lay
Silent, for oh! I could but gasp,
Till someone came that bore away
My spirit into lands unknown:

Thou, dear, who watched beside me,--say
Was it a dream from elfland blown,
Or very truth,--my doubts to stay."
"O Love, look round,--how strange and dread
The shadows of the high trees fall,
Homeward our path now let us tread,
Tomorrow I shall tell thee all.
"Arise! Be strong! Gird up thy loins!
Think of our parents, dearest friend!
The solemn darkness haste enjoins,
Not likely is it soon to end.
Hark! Jackals still at a distance howl,
The day, long, will not appear,
Lo, wild fierce eyes through bushes scowl,
Summon thy courage, lest I fear.
Was that the tiger's sullen growl?
What means this rush of many feet?
Can creatures wild so near us prowl?
Rise, and hasten homewards, sweet!"
He rose, but could not find the track,
And then, too well, Savitri knew
His wonted force had not come back.
She made a fire, and from the dew
Essayed to shelter him. At last
He nearly was himself again,--
Then vividly rose all the past,
And with the past, new fear and pain.
"What anguish must my parents feel
Who wait for me the livelong hours!
Their sore wound let us haste to heal
Before it festers, past our powers:
"For broken-hearted, they may die!
Oh hasten dear,--now I am strong,

No more I suffer, let us fly,
Ah me! each minute seems so long.
They told me once, that they could not live
Without me, in their feeble age,
Their food and water I must give
And help them in the last sad stage
Of earthly life, and that Beyond
In which a son can help by rites.
Oh, what a love is theirs--how fond!
Whom now Despair, perhaps, benights.
"Infirm herself, my mother dear
Now guides, methinks, the tottering feet
Of my blind father, for they hear
And hasten eagerly to meet
Our fancied steps. O faithful wife
Let us on wings fly back again,
Upon their safety hangs my life!"
He tried his feelings to restrain,
But like some river swelling high
They swept their barriers weak and vain,
Sudden there burst a fearful cry,
Then followed tears,--like autumn rain.
Hush! Hark, a sweet voice rises clear!
A voice of earnestness intense,
"If I have worshiped Thee in fear
And duly paid with reverence
The solemn sacrifices,--hear!
Send consolation and thy peace
Eternal, to our parents dear,
That their anxieties may cease.
Oh, ever hath I loved Thy truth,
Therefore on Thee, I dare to call,
Help us, this night, and them, forsooth

Without thy help, we perish all."
She took in hers Satyavan's hand,
She gently wiped his falling tears,
"This weakness, Love, I understand!
Courage!" She smiled away his fears.
"Now we shall go, for thou art strong."
She helped him rise by his side
And led him like a child along,
He, wistfully the basket eyed
Laden with fruit and flowers. "Not now,
Tomorrow we shall fetch it hence."
And so, she hung it on a bough,
"I'll bear thy saw for our defense."
In one fair hand, the saw she took,
The other with a charming grace
She twined around him, and her look
She turned upwards to his face.
Thus aiding him she felt anew
His bosom beat against her own--
More firm his step, more clear his view,
More self-possessed his words and tone
Became, as swift the minutes passed,
And now the pathway he discerns,
And 'neath the trees, they hurry fast,
For Hope's fair light before them burns.
Under the faint beams of the stars
How beautiful appeared the flowers,
Light scarlet, flecked with golden bars
Of the palâsas, in the bowers
That Nature there herself had made
Without the aid of man. At times
Trees on their path cast the densest shade,
And nightingales sang mystic rhymes

Their fears and sorrows to assurance.
Where two paths met, the north they chose,
As leading to the hermitage,
And soon before them, dim it rose.
    Here let us end. For all may guess
The blind old king received his sight,
And ruled again with gentleness
The country that was his by right;
And that Savitri's royal sire
Was blest with many sons,--a race
Whom poets praised for martial fire,
And every peaceful gift and grace.
As for Savitri, to this day
Her name is named, when couples wed,
And to the bride the parents say,
Be thou like her, in heart and head.

Printed by Libri Plureos GmbH in Hamburg, Germany

9 798887 720494